CALICO
THE WONDER HORSE

OR
THE SAGA OF
STEWY STINKER

STORY AND PICTURES BY VIRGINIA LEE BURTON

CALICO
THE WONDER HORSE
OR
THE SAGA OF
STEWY STINKER

STORY AND PICTURES BY
VIRGINIA LEE BURTON

Houghton Mifflin Company
Boston 1997

LC: 50-9367
RNF ISBN 0-395-85735-X   PAP ISBN 0-395-84541-6
Manufactured in the United States of America
WOZ 10 9 8 7 6 5 4 3 2 1

Way out West in Cactus County there was a horse named Calico. She wasn't very pretty . . . but she was very smart. She was the smartest fastest horse in all of Cactus County.

She could run like greased lightning and she could turn on a quarter and give you back fifteen cents in change.

She had a long and sensitive nose. She could smell like a real bloodhound. Her nose was so keen she could track a bee through a blizzard.

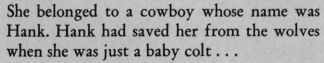

She belonged to a cowboy whose name was Hank. Hank had saved her from the wolves when she was just a baby colt . . . and Calico never forgot. She would go to the end of the trail for Hank. They had a language all their own and understood each other perfectly.

3

Everybody was happy and contented in Cactus County. There were no locks, there were no jails, and there were no fences. Twice a year they had a round-up . . . one in the Spring and one in the Fall. In the Spring the cowboys rounded up all the cattle, separated them and branded the new little calves. Hank was top cowpuncher and Calico was top cow-pony.

Across the Cactus River were the Badlands . . . good only for hideouts for Bad Men. Once a month, the stagecoach, driven by Diehard Dan, came over the narrow mountain pass, down the hairpin turns, and forded the river to bring visitors and news from the outside world to the people of Cactus County. One day Diehard Dan brought some bad news.

He had seen Stewy Stinker and his gang of Bad Men . . . Butch Bones, Snake Eye Pyezon, Buzzard Bates and little Skunk Skeeter . . . in the Badlands. Stewy Stinker was said to be so mean he would hold up Santa Claus on Christmas Eve if he had a chance. He rode a horse whose name was Mud.

They looked down on Cactus County where there were no fences, no locks and no jail, not even a Deputy Sheriff. They saw the nice fat cattle grazing peacefully on the open range.

'Ahaa!' said Stewy Stinker as he curled his long black moustache. 'Ahaa!' said he. 'Nice pickin's!'

Butch Bones was Stewy Stinker's right-hand man. Butch Bones boasted that he was so tough he would bite a live grizzly bear's nose.

Snake Eye Pyezon was Stewy Stinker's left-hand man. He was so crooked, they said, that if he swallowed nails he'd spit out corkscrews.

Buzzard Bates was so bad even a buzzard wouldn't use him for bait.

Little Skunk Skeeter just tagged along because nobody else liked him.

Stewy Stinker found a good hideout in a cave halfway up a steep mountain. Only a bloodhound could find them there and it would take an army to get them out.

The first dark night they crept quietly down from the Badlands.

They rustled a bunch of nice fat cattle from the open range. To cover their trail they drove the cattle into the river and waded upstream before going back to the Badlands.

Near their hideout was a box canyon where they hid the stolen cattle. All summer they rustled cattle from Cactus County.

'This is as easy as eating striped candy,' said Stewy Stinker, curling both his long black moustaches.

Once again it was round-up time in Cactus County. Time for the Fall round-up when they selected the beef cattle for market. The cowboys rode round and round looking for the cattle. There were few to be found. 'It must be Stewy Stinker and his gang of Bad Men who have rustled our cattle,' said Hank. 'Diehard Dan told us he was around.' The others agreed and said that he must be caught.

They posted a reward and description of Stewy Stinker. One day when Hank and Calico were reading it . . .

Calico had an idea ! ! !

She told Hank to wait for her, and raced off to the river.

She waded up and down the river sniffing right and left till she picked up Stewy Stinker's old cold trail.

To disguise herself to look like Stewy Stinker's horse she rolled over and over in the mud on the river bank.

Only a bloodhound or <u>Calico</u> could have followed Stewy Stinker's trail through the Badlands. Stewy Stinker didn't leave enough tracks to trip an ant.

When Calico reached the hideout she chased Stewy Stinker's horse, Mud, away, then quietly waited outside till Stewy Stinker came out.

He mistook her for Mud, saddled her, and got on.

Then the fireworks started. Hi! Yi! Whoopee!
High went Calico and hard she hit.

Calico bounded down the mountainside leap-
ing from rock to rock like a jack-rabbit.
Stewy Stinker pulled leather so hard he got
calluses on both hands.

18

Two whoops and a holler and they were over the river. Lightning was slow in comparison to the way they covered the country . . .

back to Hank who was waiting. Calico stopped short and unloaded Stewy Stinker

who shot through the air like a bullet.

He landed in a large patch of cacti. His yells and screams could be heard from one end of Cactus County to the other.

Calico picked Stewy Stinker out of the Cactus Patch. It would take a week to pluck him so he wouldn't look like a porcupine. The people of Cactus County gave Hank and Calico the reward. Hank did not want to take it, but Calico nodded her head and told him she had another good idea.

The idea was to give a big party for all the children in Cactus County, to be held in the schoolhouse on Christmas Eve. . . . Everybody was invited.

The next time Diehard Dan came over the mountain pass Hank went back with him to buy the presents.

As there was no jail in Cactus County, Stewy Stinker was put down in the cellar of the schoolhouse with Wishbone Bill to guard him.

Through the window Stewy Stinker heard the children talking about the mysterious and precious load that was coming in on the stagecoach. He planned to escape and hold it up.

Every night he dug up some dirt and hid it under the bed. In the daytime he covered the hole with his hat. He was digging a tunnel out of the schoolhouse cellar.

The night before the stagecoach was expected he dug the last bit and crawled out. Wishbone Bill didn't see him because he was asleep on his feet.

Stewy Stinker stole Wishbone Bill's horse and hit the trail for the Badlands.

To fool anyone who followed him he took to the tall timbers and sent Wishbone Bill's horse on.

'Well, tie my legs in a bow knot,' said Wishbone Bill when he woke up and found Stewy Stinker gone. He ran to tell the people. A Posse set out on Stewy Stinker's trail. The trail was plain to see. Calico saw the Posse go by and raced after them.

When they came to the tall timbers Calico stopped, lifted up her long and sensitive nose, and sniffed. She picked up Stewy Stinker's tall trail through the timbers and followed it . . . but the Posse kept right on following the tracks of Wishbone Bill's horse.

Stewy Stinker back in the hideout told his men of the mysterious and precious load coming in on the stagecoach that night, and his plans to hold it up in the narrow mountain pass.

Calico, hot on Stewy Stinker's trail, got there just in time to hear the plan. She had another idea, but first she must find the stolen cattle. There was no time to lose.

Meanwhile back in Cactus County, everybody from the oldest to the youngest had turned out for the party at the schoolhouse. (Everybody but the Posse who were still out looking for Stewy Stinker.) They came in their best Sunday-go-to-meetin'-clothes, in buggies, in buckboards, and in wagons. For weeks the womenfolks had been baking cakes and pies and doughnuts.

Hank off in the city had bought hundreds of presents for the children. The stagecoach was loaded high.

They got started late and knew they would have to hurry.

As they neared the Badlands the sky grew blacker and blacker. Diehard Dan cracked his whip and said, 'Looks like a real goose-drownder. We better get out of these mountains and across that river before she breaks or we'll have to wait a week.'

Meanwhile Calico had found the box canyon filled with the stolen cattle.

She let down the gate. Just then there was a blinding flash of lightning.

The cattle had been restless before. The lightning was all that was needed to start a stampede. Calico led the way.

Stewy Stinker and his gang were waiting at the narrow mountain pass.

'Here she comes!' said Stewy Stinker. 'Take your places, but hold your fire till I give the word.'

'On your marks! Get set! Fire!' Bing! Bang! Whing! Zing! Off went Hank's hat with a hole in it. Off went Diehard Dan's hat with another hole in it. 'Whoaa!' said Diehard Dan.

'Reach for the sky!' said Stewy Stinker: and Hank and Diehard Dan reached. 'I wish Calico were here,' said Hank.

'Look!' yelled Skunk Skeeter.

It was Calico at the head of the stampede. 'Run for your lives! Quick! Inside the stagecoach or you'll be trampled to death!' yelled Stewy Stinker.

Stewy Stinker grabbed the reins from Die-hard Dan. 'Giddyap!' and they were off.

'Come on! Calico!' called Hank. As Calico drew near, Hank leaped from the stagecoach to her back.

Stewy Stinker drove the stagecoach down the narrow mountain road at a breakneck speed. Hank and Calico were fast behind and the stampede thundering after them.

Inside the stagecoach Snake Eye Pyezon said, 'Whew! That was so close a shave I nearly lost my whiskers.'

Faster and faster they went. The Bad Men inside the stagecoach were being shaken around like dry peas in a pod.

Bop! Bang! Bump! Crack! 'Ouch! My head!' wailed Butch Bones as he hit the roof.

'Ouch! My nose!' cried Buzzard Bates. Poor little Skunk Skeeter couldn't say anything because he was underneath them all.

Faster and faster they raced. There was a sharp turn ahead.

Stewy Stinker reached for the brake . . . too late! One wheel went over the edge.

Diehard Dan, on the near side, leapt to safety.   over they went!
Then . . .

Hank and Calico saw them go and slid down the mountainside to look for them.

They found Stewy Stinker hanging up in a tree by his gun belt. Hank took the gun and unhooked him.

The stagecoach and horses had landed safely... without a scratch. But the rest of the Bad Men were nowhere in sight. Hank went to the door of the stagecoach and said, 'Hands up!'... No answer.

He opened the door. There they were . . . and a sad looking sight too.

Hank put Stewy Stinker inside with his Bad Men and collected all the guns. Diehard Dan got the stagecoach back on the road again.

Then the cloudburst burst!!! It rained so hard and so fast that if you opened your mouth you'd be in danger of drowning. The cattle slowed down and safely crossed the river.

Stewy Stinker looked out the window at the rain and laughed to himself. Heh! Heh! We're not caught yet. That river will be flooded in a few minutes and no one can cross it for days.

Hank and Calico knew it too. There was one chance that they could make it and they must take that chance.

They left the road, skipped the hairpin turns, and slid straight down the mountain.

At the edge of the river the stagecoach horses were frightened and refused to cross. Hank grabbed the lead horse reins and pulled them in.

Closer and closer came the wall of raging water. . . . Higher and higher rose the river. . . . Hurry! Hurry!

They just made it and raced on to the schoolhouse. On the way they passed the cattle grazing peacefully on the home range. The storm was over. The moon came out. It was a beautiful night.

When they got to the schoolhouse the children ran out to greet them and danced around Hank and Calico. 'What shall I do with the Bad Men?' said Hank to Calico. Calico had another good idea. 'Come on, boys,' said Hank, taking Calico's advice. 'This is Christmas Eve. Everybody is invited to the party. You too.'

The Bad Men were bashful. Hank loaded them up with presents and the children pulled them inside . . . all but Stewy Stinker. He sneaked out the other door of the stagecoach and peeked in the window. He saw what the mysterious and precious load was. He felt very sad.

So sad that he sat down and cried. 'I didn't know I was that mean . . . holding up Santa Claus on Christmas Eve. I'm never going to be bad any more.'

Calico found him and persuaded him to go inside and join the others.

Inside Stewy Stinker saw Buzzard Bates get hit on the nose by a jack-in-the-box and laughed and laughed. Butch Bones was pretending he was a grizzly bear and let the children ride on his back . . . Snake Eye Pyezon was playing dolls and Skunk Skeeter was having the time of his life because everybody liked him.

Young Wishbone Bill asked Stewy Stinker to play trains with him and soon they were all having a good time. When the Posse got back and found Stewy Stinker and his Bad Men playing with toys on the floor with the children they could hardly believe their eyes.

Everybody had such a good time at the party that it lasted till New Year's Day, and then the Bad Men promised to be good. Hank was elected Sheriff of Cactus County and Calico was made his Deputy Sheriff. They all shook hands and once again everybody was happy and contented in Cactus County.

Publisher's Note: A Symphony in Comics

First published in 1941, *Calico the Wonder Horse or The Saga of Stewy Stinker* was ahead of its time. In fact, so much so that this publisher selected the more reserved subtitle of *The Saga of Stewy Slinker.* Not until the 1950 revised edition was Stewy's surname reinstated to Burton's original preference of Stinker. (A tongue-in-cheek tribute to Stewy's pseudonym appears on the WANTED poster on page fourteen.) Yet the somewhat controversial title was secondary to Burton's progressive sense of design and her use of the comic-strip format.

Always one to write for a specific audience — her two sons — Burton began to write a book about cars that found her oldest son, Aris, at age nine, unenthusiastic. In an article in the July–August 1941 issue of *The Horn Book Magazine* titled "Symphony in Comics," she observes what her son did find enticing: "The comics, the funnies, and the radio programs absorbed him completely; not only him but all the other boys his age. Here was something to look into. What was it that held them so enthralled? Comic books were like currency. They could be traded for toys. They were collected like treasures. There must be a reason for it.

"I soon found out that these books and programs satisfied a natural craving for excitement . . . action . . . drama; gave the children a hero to worship and an escape to thrilling adventure that is wanted by any normal child. . . . The hero must be endowed with more than the average physical and mental powers, besides being all that was chivalrous and virtuous, and the villain the anitithesis. . . . There must be action, suspense, and tremendous but possible odds against the hero, but no one must get seriously hurt. Humor was welcome. Westerns were the most popular."

Understanding these elements and following a cue from those in the West who say "When in doubt, trust to yo' hoss," Burton created a saga with the central character Calico, The Wonder Horse. In the *Horn Book* article she shares the application of her design sense: "I had been working on design and now had a chance to use it. In design, movement is opposed to monotony. The circle or half circle is at rest. Developed into a spiral, it moves. A right angle is stationary. A slight variation in degree and it immediately takes on life. My book began to be what my family called a 'symphony in comics.'"

In addition to creating movement and mood with angles, spirals, and circles, Burton selected the pages' colors to accentuate her storytelling. Soft pastels illustrate the quiet life in Cactus County, but when the scene shifts, the hues darken. Bright colors bring the story to a climax; while blue, during a violent storm, starts the denouement. And then, a happy ending with a soft yellow.

In order to compete with what she called the "lurid tales" on the market in 1941, Burton knew she couldn't be a complete reactionary. In creating *Calico the Wonder Horse or The Saga of Stewy Stinker,* she indeed proved to be quite original, paving the way for future works which incorporate graphic design into fiction.